Meet the Weirds

by

Kaye Umansky

Illustrated by Chris Mould

You do not need to read this page – just get on with the book!

First published in 2003 in Great Britain by
Barrington Stoke Ltd
18 Walker Street, Edinburgh, EH3 7LP

www.barringtonstoke.co.uk

Reprinted 2004 (twice), 2005, 2006, 2008

ISBN: 978-1-84299-114-5

Printed in Great Britain by Bell & Bain Ltd

MEET THE AUTHOR – KAYE UMANSKY

What is your favourite animal?
Cat
What is your favourite boy's name?
Ethan
What is your favourite girl's name?
Ella
What is your favourite food?
Cheese, but I mustn't
What is your favourite music?
Soul
What is your favourite hobby?
Reading in bed

MEET THE ILLUSTRATOR – CHRIS MOULD

What is your favourite animal?
Lizard
What is your favourite boy's name?
Chris! It's so cool, like me.
What is your favourite girl's name?
Emily and Charlotte (my two daughters)
What is your favourite food?
Curry
What is your favourite music?
I love all kinds of music
What is your favourite hobby?
Drawing!

To Mo and Ella

Contents

Chapter 1
The Weirds Arrive

The day the Weirds moved in to Number 17 Tidy Street, Mrs Primm called in to say hello. Well, that's why she said she came. Really, she was just being nosy.

Number 17 had been empty for a long time. Mrs Primm stood on the doorstep, shaking her head at the shocking state of the garden. It let the street down. She must have a word about that. And that awful, old tree out the back, which was blocking off all her light.

The new family had arrived in the night, which was odd. Mrs Primm knew they were there, though. There was an upturned shopping trolley under a bush and bits of string and empty boxes all over the place. Smoke was coming from the chimney.

Mrs Primm wanted a word about that as well. Tidy Street was a Smokeless Zone. No open fires were allowed.

She gave a brisk rap with the knocker. Flakes of old paint rained down on her shoes.

There was a long pause. Then came the sound of unsteady footsteps. Then, scuffling noises. Then, heavy breathing. Slowly, the door opened. The dirty face of a very small child looked out.

"Is your mummy in, dear?" asked Mrs Primm, peering in. The dark and gloomy hall was full of boxes and crates. From somewhere in the back, there came a crashing noise and then the splintering of glass. Something big was throwing itself at a door.

The small child just stared and said nothing. He was standing on a packing case, wobbling a bit. He wore a fireman's helmet, hamster slippers and a drooping nappy. His nose was running.

"If you'll just get Mummy?" said Mrs Primm, and waited.

Still nothing, except the hard stare.

"What's your name, dear?" asked Mrs Primm, sweetly.

"His name's Frankly and he's not allowed to open the door," said a voice from inside. "Get down, Frankly. Or else."

Mrs Primm saw a girl with bird's nest hair, topped with a floppy hat trimmed with fake grapes. She had an old, orange curtain draped round her and was wearing yellow wellingtons.

"Is your mother in, dear?" asked Mrs Primm. "I'm Mrs Primm from Number 15."

"She's out jumping from an aeroplane. Get *down*, Frankly," said the girl.

Frankly got down from the packing case and gave Mrs Primm another Look. Then he turned, pulled up his nappy and trotted off down the hall.

"I'm sorry," said Mrs Primm. "Did you say – jumping from an aeroplane?"

"She's a stunt woman. She stands in for filmstars when they're too scared to do things themselves."

"I see," said Mrs Primm, in a faint voice. "I *see*. Er – is anyone else home?"

"Dad's in the cellar. It's more than our life's worth to go Down There." She pointed down some steep, stone steps.

There was something very creepy about the way she said this.

"So is there nobody grown-up around, then?" asked Mrs Primm.

"Well, there's Gran. She's not exactly grown-up, though."

"I beg your pardon?"

"She's a dwarf," said the girl.

"Oh. *Oh!* I'm sorry, I didn't ..."

"It's all right, she likes it. Anyway, she's frying chips. It's not a good time to speak to her. I could get my brother Oliver, but he's doing his homework. Why don't you try again tomorrow?"

"Thank you," said Mrs Primm. "I will. I just wanted a little chat about dustbins and fire laws and things. And perhaps your father could do something about that awful, old tree at the back ...?"

But she was talking to the door.

She was wondering whether to slip a note through the letterbox when there came a big thump from the other side. The door rattled in its frame. Claws scraped the wood. There was a deep-throated snarl.

She hurried away down the path.

Chapter 2
The Primms

It was evening, and the Primms were eating their dinner. Mr and Mrs Primm liked sitting at a proper table in a proper manner with their son, Pinchton. They usually had soup, followed by fish with the head still on and salad. For pudding, there was healthy grapefruit.

"Eat your radish, Pinchton," said Mrs Primm. "Stop pushing it under your fish. I can see, you know."

"Sorry, Mother," said Pinchton. He speared the radish with his fork and took a small bite.

"How was your day, dear?" asked Mr Primm. He had just got home. He wanted to get the family news out of the way so that he could do the crossword puzzle.

"Oh, you know. A woman's work is never done. I called in to say hello to the new people next door," Mrs Primm told him.

"Oh? What are they like?" her husband asked.

"Odd. I didn't meet the parents. I just saw two of the children. More salad?"

"No, thanks. So how are they odd?"

"I don't know. They're – wild-looking. Like they've been reared by wolves. The mother does *stunts*, of all things. And the grandma is – well – a dwarf."

"A *dwarf*?"Mr Primm raised his eyebrows.

"So the girl told me. And I'm very much afraid there's a dog. A big one, by the sound of it. I don't want you playing with them, Pinchton."

"Pardon, Mother?" said Pinchton.

"You're not to play with the new children next door. Just be polite, then firmly walk away."

"All right," said Pinchton. "May I leave the table, please?"

"Don't you want your grapefruit?" asked his mother.

"No, thanks. I'm full."

"Well, all right. Are you going to tidy your room?"

"It's tidy."

"Have you folded your pyjamas?"

"Yes."

"Well, there's a bird programme on TV about the Great Bustard. Do you want to watch it with Daddy and me? As a special treat?"

"Come to think of it," said Pinchton, "come to think of it, I don't think my room *is* quite tidy. I think I might have left a pair of socks out."

"Pinchton!" cried his mother. "What are drawers for? Go and put them away. Oh, before you do, pop out and give my tomatoes a water, will you? Not too much. Just half a can. With a pinch of the pink plant food."

"The pink plant food," nodded Pinchton. "I know."

"Good boy. Don't walk on the grass in your shoes. And wipe your feet when you come back in."

****

Pinchton stepped into the back garden with the watering can. It was a fine evening, with a cool breeze. Birds sang in the cherry tree. Bill and Ben, the two goldfish, swam in bored circles around the ornamental pond. Around it stood a model windmill, a plastic heron and a tribe of garden gnomes armed with fishing rods. Three of the rods were broken, he noticed. Strange.

He was just tipping up the can to water the tomatoes when:

"Oi!" said a voice. "Over here!"

Pinchton looked up. A girl was staring at him over the neatly clipped hedge. He could only see her head. She was wearing a hat with fruit on.

"Um – hello," said Pinchton in a polite voice.

"I'm Ott," said the girl.

"Are you? I'm quite chilly, myself."

"No. Ott. Short for Otterly. That's my name. Otterly Weird."

Pinchton thought to himself that this was a very strange name. But he was too polite to say so.

"Mmm," he said. "I've never heard that name before."

"We've just moved in," said Ott. "Who are you?"

"Pinchton Primm," said Pinchton. He gave an uneasy look back at the house.

"Oh, *right*. Your mum called round."

"Yes – um – yes."

"Come closer," said Ott. "I want to talk to you."

"It's all right," said Pinchton. "I'm fine over here."

"Why are you wearing that coat?" Ott asked him.

"It's a blazer. School uniform."

"But it's Saturday," Ott pointed out.

"Mother and Father like me to look smart at the dinner table."

"Crikey," said Ott. "I'm glad *we* don't have to wear anything like that."

"You will if you go to my school," said Pinchton, in a prim voice. "It's the rule."

"Really?" said Ott. "We're not great ones for rules in our house. Do you want to come over? I'm making a den for Frankly."

"Sorry," said Pinchton. "I'm busy. Anyway, there's a hedge between us."

"We've made a hole in it," Ott told him. "At the bottom, down by your compost heap. Come and have a look."

A hole? *In the hedge?* Whatever would his mother say?

"I really can't," said Pinchton

"Why not?" the girl asked.

"I have to water the tomatoes."

"So get a move on. Meet you at the hole."

With that, the head vanished.

Pinchton quickly poured the water into the pots. He was just about to hurry back inside when the Weird girl's voice came again from the bottom of the garden.

"Pinch! Down here!" she called.

Pinchton put down the can and looked around. Nobody was looking. His parents were watching the Great Bustard on TV.

He hurried off down the path.

Chapter 3
Through the Hole

Pinchton was relieved to see that the hole in the hedge was quite small. If he stuck a couple of gnomes in front, maybe his mother wouldn't notice it.

"Are you coming or what?" hissed Ott.

Pinchton took off his blazer and placed it neatly on the grass. He bent down and wriggled through the hole.

The Weird girl was waiting for him. Fruit hat. Orange curtain. Yellow wellies. Hmm.

He brushed the leaves from his shirt, then stared around. He had never been in Number 17's garden. His mother said there might be snakes.

Snakes? *Lions*, more like. It was a complete jungle. You couldn't tell where the flowerbeds ended and the grass began. The awful, old tree grew slap-bang in the middle of the garden. Its lower branches sagged down to the ground.

"Great, isn't it?" said Ott, cheerfully. "What do you think of the den?"

She pointed to a low branch. Smaller branches had been propped against it on either side, so it was a bit like a tent.

"It's good," nodded Pinchton.

"Frankly's inside cooking dinner. It's just pretend. Do you want to say hello?"

"Look, I can't stay long," said Pinchton with a nervous look over his shoulder.

"It won't take a minute. Shove up, Frankly! I'm coming in – with Pinch!"

Ott dropped on her hands and knees and crawled under the tree. After a moment, Pinchton followed.

It was crowded in the den. Frankly was crouched in the leafy gloom, using a stick to stir something in an old paint tin. There were three large, flat, yellow flower heads laid out on the grass in front of him.

Pinchton went cold. He knew those flowers. He had seen them before.

"Um," he said, pointing. "Um – those sunflowers. Where did you get them?"

"From your garden," said Ott. "That's why we made the hole. They're Frankly's dinner plates. He liked your goldfish too, didn't you, Frankly?"

Frankly went on stirring the old paint tin and said nothing. He was wearing hamster slippers and a grass-stained nappy. Did nobody dress normally in this family?

"He liked the garden gnomes too," went on Ott. "He liked snapping off their fishing rods."

Aaah.

Pinchton was terribly shocked. Not only had these Weird kids made a hole into his garden, they had helped themselves to flowers and trashed the place. What if his mum had seen them?

"I've really got to go," he said. He had been polite. Now was the time to walk away.

"You can go after dinner. Come on, Frankly, we're hungry."

Frankly stopped stirring, held the tin up high and poured out the contents. To Pinchton's horror, thick, black mud mixed with grass and pebbles plopped down onto his mother's sunflowers!

Some of it splashed onto his shirt!

"Oops," said Ott, with a giggle. "Steady on, Frankly. Now see what you've done."

"My shirt!" wailed Pinchton. "Look at it! My mother'll go mad!"

"Sorry," said Ott. "Here, I'll rub it with grass."

"No, no! Don't! You're only making it worse!" cried Pinchton.

"Okay, okay, calm down," said Ott. "No, Frankly, no more. Put the tin *down* ..."

Too late. More of the disgusting stuff plopped down, this time on Pinchton's trousers. He stared at the dark stains in horror.

"Tell you what," said Ott. "We'll go in and see Gran. She'll get it off. As you mind so much."

"No," said Pinchton, stiffly. "No, it's all right."

"No, really. She will. What sign are you?" asked Ott.

"What do you mean?"

"Star sign. There's some she doesn't like. What are you?"

"I don't know. We don't believe in that sort of thing in our house," said Pinchton, a bit stiffly.

"When's your birthday?"

"Twenty-third of April," said Pinchton.

"Taurus. The sign of the Bull. You're okay. She's frying more chips. You can have some if you like. Or there's wedding cake. You can meet Dad, if he's up."

"*Up*?" said Pinchton in surprise.

"From the cellar. He's working on an invention. Mum's not back yet and Oliver's doing homework."

"Homework? On a Saturday?"

"Yep. He likes it. He does extra on Saturdays."

Pinchton was speechless. A boy who liked doing extra homework? On Saturdays? How weird was that?

"And you can meet Ginger," Ott went on.

"Is that the dog?"

"We don't have a dog. Come on."

Ott began crawling out of the den. Her curtain trailed through Frankly's horrible dinner, but she didn't appear to notice.

"Are you coming?" Pinchton asked Frankly, a little crossly. In reply, Frankly picked up a handful of muddy flowers and began rubbing them into his hair.

"Come *on*," Ott said to Pinchton.

With a hopeless shrug he followed.

COOKING OIL

Chapter 4
Gran

"This is Pinch, Gran," said Ott. "Frankly dropped mud on him."

The Weirds' kitchen was like nothing Pinchton had ever seen. There was no sign of any of the usual kitchen stuff – cooker, fridge, washing machine and so on. Just boxes and piles of pots and pans dumped just anywhere. And a strange sort of plant in a pot which seemed to have nothing but stalks and tendrils.

A large, black cat sat on the draining board, its nose buried in a saucepan. It spat as Pinchton entered, then went back to eating. The only item of furniture was a table, on which sat a large, iced wedding cake with three tiers. A slice was missing from the top layer.

The strangest thing of all, though, was Gran. She had a big, hooked nose and a sucked-in mouth. She wore a black shawl and tiny boots with buttons up the side. The top of her head only came to Pinchton's shoulder.

She stood over a huge, sizzling pan, frying chips in the fireplace. There was a big sack of potatoes, a pile of peelings and a giant-sized bottle of cooking oil. On the floor was a sheet of newspaper, overflowing with chips she had fried earlier. There was enough to feed an army.

"What sign are you?" she demanded, staring up at Pinchton with eyes like blackcurrants.

"Taurus," said Pinchton at once. He was glad Ott had warned him.

"The Bull. Solid. Sensible. But you can be stubborn. Right, get 'em off."

"Get what off?"

"Your clothes. You want 'em cleanin', don't you?"

"Um –"

"So get 'em off."

"I'll get you one of Oliver's jumpers," said Ott, and tactfully left the room.

Pinchton wasn't sure, but he thought the peculiar plant swayed towards her as she went past.

He took off his shirt and stepped out of his trousers. He felt shy and a bit silly.

He passed the muddy clothes to Gran, who snatched them away and took them over to the sink. She pulled out a box and climbed on it. Water glugged from the tap and clouds of steam rose.

"Have a chip," shouted Gran, over her shoulder.

Pinchton looked down at the floor. Ten minutes ago he was a normal boy. Now, he was in a dwarf's kitchen *in his underwear*, facing a chip mountain.

The Primms didn't eat chips. Too greasy. Too unhealthy. Too common.

Oh well, thought Pinchton. *So what*? He took a small one and bit into it. It was wonderful.

"I'm not looking," said Ott, coming back in with her hand over her eyes. She had something brown and woolly in her hand.

The plant reached out a long, green waving tendril and sort of sniffed her as she passed. It really did! Pinchton was sure of it this time.

Gratefully, Pinchton took the brown jumper and pulled it on. It came down to his ankles. Oliver must be very tall.

Ott helped herself to a handful of chips and leaned against the table, munching.

"Have some," she said. "There's loads."

"Thanks. Really? Wow. Um – you don't have a plate, by any chance?" asked Pinchton.

"Crikey," said Ott. "Hear that, Gran? He's asking for a plate."

A cackle of laughter came from where Gran was standing at the sink.

“We don’t bother with plates,” Ott explained. “We usually eat straight from the pan. Saves on washing-up. Just dig in.”

Pinchton dug in.

“Dad’s still in the cellar, then?” Ott asked Gran, into the cloud of steam.

“Yep,” said Gran. “I’ve taken down his chips.”

“It must be interesting having an inventor for a father,” said Pinchton, wistfully. Mr Primm was a deputy bank manager. “What’s he working on?”

“It’s a secret. We won’t know until he’s finished.”

“And when will that be?” asked Pinchton.

"Who knows? Usually when the house blows up."

"Ha, ha," laughed Pinchton, weakly, and stuffed in a few more chips. He hoped she was joking.

"Good chips, eh?" said Ott.

"Fantastic."

"We have them every day," Ott told him.

Chips every day? Pinchton couldn't believe his own ears.

"They're the only thing we all like," explained Ott. "We're funny about food. Oliver likes wedding cake. Ginger and Frankly like pink custard. Gran doesn't eat. Mum likes meat. Dad likes stuffed tomatoes and *I* like sweets. What do *you* like, Pinch?"

Pinchton thought about this. "Well," he said finally, "I *think* I like all those things. But I know what I *don't* like. Fish with the head still on."

"Quite right too," said Gran, from over by the sink. "Never eat nothin' that stares back at you. Where's Frankly, Ott?"

"In his den. Rubbing mud into his hair," replied Ott.

"Well, it's time he came in. Your mum'll be back soon. She'll expect him to be watching rubbish on the telly, not out there catchin' his death of cold."

"Um – what sort of stunts does your mum do?" Pinchton wanted to know.

"Daring dives. Driving cars over cliffs. Grappling with sharks. Anything really dangerous. She could meet her death any day."

"Sharks, eh?" nodded Pinchton. "Well, well. Wow." *His* mother spent most of her time tidying the house and garden.

Suddenly, from somewhere in the house came an ear-splitting crash, then a snarl.

Pinchton nearly jumped out of the huge jumper. "Eek!" he gasped. "What was that? Ginger?"

"No. *That's* Ginger," said Ott, pointing at the black cat on the windowsill.

"So what was snarling ...?"

Just then, Gran scuttled over from the sink. In her tiny hands were Pinchton's shirt and trousers, tidily hung on a hanger. To his amazement, they were perfectly clean!

Not a mark on them. What's more, they were bone dry and looked as though they had been ironed!

"See?" said Ott. "I said she'd fix them."

"Thanks," Pinchton said, in a weak voice. "That's – amazing."

"Don't put 'em on straight away," Gran told him. "You don't want to get 'em mucked up, going through that hole. Borrow Oliver's jumper, he won't mind."

"Right," said Pinchton. "Very kind of you. Well, I suppose I should be getting back."

"Want a bit of cake before you go?" asked Ott.

Pinchton was tempted. But he wanted to get back before anyone noticed he was missing.

"No, thank you," he said. "I'm full of chips."

"Stay and meet Mum," urged Ott. "She'll be back soon."

The shark grappler? Hmm.

"No," he said. "I really have to go."

"Another time, then," said Gran.

"Yes. Yes, thank you very much," said Pinchton politely.

"See you, Pinch," said Ott.

"See you, Ott," said Pinchton.

And, rather unwillingly, he went home.

Chapter 5
Oliver

It was Sunday morning. Mr and Mrs Primm had gone to a garden centre to buy more gnomes. They had wanted to take Pinchton, but he had used homework as an excuse. In fact, he didn't have any homework, but he could do without the excitement of a gnome-buying trip. Besides, there was something he needed to do.

He rapped the knocker of Number 17, hoping the Weirds were up. There was no knowing. For all he knew, they lay in coffins all day and got up at sunset.

There was something new in the front garden. It was a large, oily motorbike. Pinchton sighed. He was sure his mum would have *plenty* to say about that.

After a long wait, he heard shuffling footsteps.

"What?" shouted a cross voice. "Who is it?"

"Me. Pinchton from next door."

The door opened a crack. A pale, spotty face topped with floppy hair peered out through thick, owlish glasses.

"Hello," said Pinchton. "I hope I'm not too early?"

"For what?" said the spotty face.

"To return this jumper." Pinchton held up the huge, brown garment. The strange boy stared at it.

"It's mine," he said.

Ah! This must be Oliver. Spooky Homework Boy.

"Yes," said Pinchton. "I borrowed it. Bit of a problem with my own clothes. Anyway, thanks for the loan. Here."

He stuffed the jumper into Oliver's hands.

"Do you want to come in?" said Oliver.

Pinchton thought. Did he? Well, yes, he did.

"Thanks," he said. "Just for a minute, then."

Once inside, he realised how incredibly tall and thin Oliver was. He towered over Pinchton like a telegraph pole. He wore a green anorak on top and blue pyjama bottoms down below. His long, white feet were stuffed into enormous, green sandals. What was it with this family's footwear?

"Everyone's in bed," said Oliver. "They stayed up all night celebrating. I didn't. Needed an early start. Maths homework to do."

"Right," nodded Pinchton. "Good for you. Um – what were they celebrating?"

"Dad's finished his invention."

So *that's* what all the racket was about last night. The cheering and the singing. His mother claimed that she hadn't slept a wink.

"Want to come up to my room?" asked Oliver.

"Right," said Pinchton. "Um – after you."

Oliver's attic room was filthy beyond belief. Pinchton gasped. His mother would have had a fit. Unmade bed, piles of dirty clothes, odd shoes – and books *everywhere*. The ones that wouldn't fit on the crowded shelves were piled on the floor. On the rumpled bed, rising from a sea of icing crumbs, was the wedding cake, minus the top layer.

PROFESSOR
STEPHEN
HAWKING
INK

The walls were bare except for a world map and a poster of Stephen Hawking, the famous scientist. The table was cluttered. There was a globe, a microscope, a quill pen, a bottle of ink, a million chewed pencils and several enormous towers of paper covered in spidery writing.

There was enough there to keep a teacher marking until the end of time. You could see that Oliver took his homework very seriously indeed.

"Cake?" asked Oliver.

"Um – yes, please."

Oliver scrabbled around, found a pair of scissors, hacked off a lump and handed it to Pinchton without a word.

"Is that your mum's bike in your front garden?" Pinchton asked, taking a greedy bite. He loved fruitcake.

"Yep. It's a Harley-Davidson."

"And she really grapples with sharks?"

"Not when she's on the bike."

A little silence fell. Pinchton munched his cake. Oliver sat and fiddled with a pencil.

"It's great your father's finished his invention," said Pinchton.

"Yep."

"And the house hasn't blown up, ha, ha?"

"Not this time," Oliver nodded.

"Right. Good. Um – what is it?"

"A rocket-propelled back pack. It's a present for Mum. Extra thrust when she's diving off things," Oliver told him.

"Wow!"

Pinchton was impressed. *His* mum got perfume for her birthday.

Suddenly, there was another loud crash downstairs.

"What *is* that?" asked Pinchton. He wanted to get to the bottom of these strange noises.

"Gran's best marzipan," said Oliver as Pinchton bit into another slice of cake.

"No, I mean those noises I keep hearing."

"Ah," said Oliver, "well that's ..."

"*Oliver!*" bellowed a voice from far below.

"What?"

"Gran's doing chips. Do you want some?"

"No! I'm trying to work up here!"

"Is Frankly up with you? He's missing again," went on the voice.

"No!"

"All right, just checking."

Pinchton raised an enquiring eyebrow. "Is that your mum?"

"Yes." Oliver was fiddling with his quill pen. He was clearly keen to get back to his homework.

Pinchton stood up. "Well," he said, "thanks for the cake. I'll find my own way out."

"Mmm," said Oliver, "bye." He had already dipped the quill in the ink and was busy scribbling.

Pinchton hurried down the stairs. He would just let himself out quietly without bothering anyone. He was just about to open the front

door, when a big, powerful woman with wild, orange hair came striding out of the kitchen. She wore a leather jacket, leather trousers and pink cowboy boots. She was eating a chicken drumstick. She stopped in surprise when she saw Pinchton.

"Hello, boy," she boomed loudly. "You're not one of mine, are you? If you are, I can't remember having you."

"Ha, ha," tittered Pinchton. "No, I'm Pinchton Primm from next door. I was just bringing back Oliver's jumper."

"Ah, yes! Ott's little friend. Want some chips?"

"Thanks, but I'd better be getting home," said Pinchton. He didn't know how long his parents would be away. He didn't want to be caught coming out of Number 17.

"Please yourself. I'll tell Ott you called."

"Thanks, Mrs Weird," said Pinchton. And he hurried back home.

Chapter 6
Complaining

It was the following Saturday morning. Pinchton sat in his perfectly tidy bedroom, playing a racing game on his PlayStation 2. His parents didn't approve, but his Uncle Ted had given it to him for his last birthday, so they couldn't say much.

All last week, Pinchton had half expected Ott and Oliver to turn up at his school, but they hadn't. Perhaps they were going to another school. Perhaps they didn't go to school at all. Either way, he found he was a bit disappointed. He had crept out into the garden every evening and peeped over the hedge, but there had been no sign of the Weirds. Maybe they were away.

Suddenly, he heard a loud cry from the garden below. He peered out of the window. His mother was standing by the ornamental pond. He saw his father come out to join her, holding the paper. They started talking and pointing down at the water. Then they looked up at Pinchton's bedroom window.

"Come down here, please, Pinchton!" his mother ordered.

With a sigh, Pinchton went down and joined them in the garden.

"Yes, Mother?" he said.

"Bill and Ben are missing."

“Crikey,” said Pinchton. “Are they?”

“Don’t say that horrid word. Do you know anything about this?”

“No, of course not,” said Pinchton.

“What *is* going on here?” demanded his mother. “First, the heads of the sunflowers are missing. Then the gnomes’ dear little rods are broken ...”

"I was thinking about that. Maybe Bill and Ben jumped up and bit them off?" suggested Pinchton. "As a sort of fish protest. And then died from all that effort."

"Don't be ridiculous, son," said his father.

"Well, let's face it, it's a pretty boring pond," said Pinchton.

"You're talking rubbish."

"Well, *something's* happened to them! They've gone, haven't they?" wailed Mrs Primm.

"There, there," soothed Mr Primm. "Look on the bright side. Your tomatoes are doing well."

"It's that cat!" snapped Mrs Primm. "That evil, black cat from next door."

"His name's Ginger," said Pinchton, without thinking.

"What?" said his parents together.

"Um – I heard them calling him."

"Why is a black cat called Ginger?"

"Ha, ha. I don't know."

"Anyway," said Mrs Primm, firmly, "anyway, I'm going in to complain about it. *Right now.* It's time I had a word with the Weirds. About a *lot* of things. That dreadful motorbike, for a start. Did you hear the noise last night? And they *still* haven't done a thing about that awful, old tree."

"Listen," said Pinchton, desperate not to get the Weirds into trouble. "Listen. It might not have been the cat. It might have been a – a passing penguin or something."

"Is the boy mad?" asked Mr Primm.

"I'm just saying. You shouldn't accuse them unless you're sure they did it."

"That's quite enough, Pinchton. This is grown-up business," said Mrs Primm. She had the light of battle in her eyes. She turned to her husband. "Are you coming, my dear?"

"I think it's perhaps better if one of us goes, don't you?" said Mr Primm. He was longing to get back to his crossword. "And you're very good at this sort of thing," he added, to be on the safe side.

"Right. I shall see you shortly," Mrs Primm told them.

****

She was back in five minutes.

"How did it go, my dear?" asked Mr Primm, from behind the crossword.

Pinchton held his breath and waited. He was dreading what his mum would say.

"They've invited us to a barbecue," said Mrs Primm, faintly. "Tonight. Put the kettle on, Pinchton, I need a cup of mint tea."

"A barbecue?" Mr Primm's eyebrows shot through the roof. "What – *meat*?"

"Yes, I explained we only eat fish. Isa said that would be fine."

"Isa?" said Mr Primm looking confused.

"That's her name. She insisted I call her it. She was very – friendly. Strange clothes, but – friendly."

"Did you mention the bike?" asked her husband.

"Yes. She said she was sorry and it wouldn't happen again. Oh, and by the way, the cat didn't eat the goldfish. It's a fussy eater. It only likes one thing."

"Pink custard," muttered Pinchton under his breath.

"What?" said his mother.

"A Great Bustard," Pinchton said. "I've seen one circling round. That's what took poor old Bill and Ben, I expect."

Pinchton saw his father looking at him. "It's all right, I'll shut up now," he said, feebly.

"And the tree?" Mr Primm asked his wife. "Did you mention that?"

"Funnily enough, I didn't get round to it."

"That's not like you, my dear."

"I know. But she was so very – friendly."

Chapter 7
A Mystery Solved

Ott, Frankly and Pinchton were sitting on the grass under the awful, old tree. Oliver was in his room, doing homework. Mr Weird was down in the cellar, starting a new invention. Mrs Weird and Gran were shouting cheerfully to each other in the kitchen. They were preparing for the evening's barbecue.

"So what have you done with the goldfish, Frankly?" asked Ott, sternly.

Frankly was wearing a homemade squirrel suit with a bushy tail. Someone had drawn felt-tip whiskers on his dirty cheeks. He nibbled a paw and said nothing.

"Come on. Own up. We know it was you," Ott went on.

"Perhaps it *wasn't* him," said Pinchton, trying to be fair.

Pinchton was supposed to be indoors polishing his shoes for the party in the evening. His father was doing the crossword and his mother was lying down in her bedroom. It had been the work of moments to slip through the hole. He had found Ott and Frankly collecting wood for a bonfire.

They had been pleased to see him until he mentioned the missing fish.

"Of course it was him," said Ott. "He takes things. Frankly, have you put them in a bucket?"

Silence.

"In the bath?"

Silence.

"Not – *in your potty*?"

Frankly said nothing but gave Ott a withering Look.

"Did you put them in the pond?" demanded Ott.

Pinchton was startled. A pond? There was *a pond* at Number 17?

"If you don't tell, there'll be trouble," warned Ott. "I'll tell the Plant to slurp you. You know you hate that."

A big tear slid down Frankly's cheek. He wiped it away, smearing his whiskers. Slowly, he nodded.

"Come on," said Ott, standing up and holding out her hand. "Show us. It's all right, we're not cross."

"I am a bit," said Pinchton. He was fond of Bill and Ben. Filled with guilt, Frankly sobbed into his bushy squirrel's tail. "But as long as they're all right, it's okay," Pinchton added, quickly.

Frankly cheered up.

****

There was a pond all right. It was a dark, deep, cool place in a secret corner, edged with ferns and covered with lily pads. Down below, in the green depths, he saw a flicker of gold. Then another.

"There they are! I see them!"

"Sorry, Pinch," said Ott. "We'll catch them and bring them back. Somehow."

"It's all right," said Pinchton. "If I was them, I know which pond I'd like best. Just don't say anything to my mother at the barbecue tonight. Look, I've got to go."

"Okay. See you later," said Ott. "I'm looking forward to the party, aren't you?"

In fact, Pinchton was dreading it. Goodness knows what a Weird barbecue would be like. What would his parents make of the house? The Plant? Gran? Oliver? The Cake? The Chips? The Thudding Thing That Snarls?

Even worse, his mother was trying to make him wear his blazer!

Chapter 8
The Barbecue

"Where were you all week?" Pinchton asked Ott. "I kept looking, but until today, you weren't there."

It was evening and the party was in full swing. They were sitting on a branch of the awful, old tree.

For once, Ott was dressed in a T-shirt and jeans. If it wasn't for the fact that she was still wearing the fruit hat, she could almost pass for normal. The hat, and the message on her T-shirt: I'M WEIRD, ME.

"We went to the mountains. To try out Dad's new invention. And Frankly wandered off and Mum had to do a Search and Rescue to find him. But you'll see plenty of us from now on. We're starting at your school on Monday. This is fun, eating up a tree, isn't it?"

"Yep," said Pinchton, through a mouthful of wedding cake. In his lap was a floppy cardboard plate full of chips, with pink custard on the side. Much to his relief, his mother had given in to him over the blazer and let him wear his football strip.

"Are they enjoying themselves, do you think?" asked Ott. "Your mum and dad?"

Pinchton stared down at his parents, who were sitting on a packing case, tucking into fish. “Well, yes,” he said, “yes, I think they are.”

****

“Do you think Pinchton should be up in that tree?” said Mrs Primm, suddenly. “He might fall.”

“Do him good,” said her husband. “Spends too much time on his own. Don’t want him weak and wimpish. I always climbed trees when I was a lad. Great fun. Fell out of ’em too. Didn’t do me any harm.”

“Mmm,” said Mrs Primm. “Of course, it *does* block the light. But perhaps you’re right. Maybe if they just trim it a little.”

“I could do it,” offered Mr Primm. “Wouldn’t take long, with the electric saw.”

"That would be nice." Mrs Primm took her husband's arm and gazed at the raging bonfire. "You know, there's nothing like a good, old-fashioned blaze, is there? Reminds me of being a Girl Guide."

"Were you a Guide?" asked Mr Primm. "You never told me."

"Oh yes. I had badges. Such a novel idea, a barbecue over a bonfire. This fish is rather good, isn't it? And the stuffed tomatoes are delicious. I wonder where they got them? Home-grown, by the taste."

She stood up. "Where are you going?" asked her husband.

"To see if I can help, of course. I'm sure Isa could do with a hand." Mr Primm waited until his wife's back was turned, then headed for the chips.

Up in the tree, Pinchton breathed a sigh of relief. For once, his parents hadn't embarrassed him.

He looked down at the scene below him. Tiny Gran with her frying pan. His father, sneaking chips. Mrs Weird, shouting and laughing her orange head off, striding about in her pink boots with huge amounts of food. His mother, going over to talk to her. Oliver, sitting on a chair, doing his homework. Frankly, doing terrible things with fire in a corner. Ginger, the black cat, prowling around by the secret pond.

No sign of The Plant, thank goodness. That had stayed indoors. It must be a House Plant.

Mr Weird was there, too, to complete the family circle. He had finally come up from the cellar to take his place as Master of the Barbecue. He was just what Pinchton had

expected – mad scientist hair, milk bottle glasses and bandaged fingers. He even wore a white lab coat, covered with burns and stains. Right now, he had put on a plastic apron and was waving about an enormous pair of tongs.

The barbecue itself was a truly Weird affair consisting of old, iron gates welded together. The whole thing looked as if it had been struck by lightning. Another of Mr Weird's inventions, Pinchton suspected.

Pinchton suddenly thought of something. "Ott," he said. "I've been meaning to ask. You know those strange, crashing noises in your house? And the snarling?"

"Yes?" she said.

"Um – what *is* it, exactly?"

"Ah," said Ott. "Well, of course, that's ..."

"Ott!" came her mother's voice from below the tree. "Go and take those matches off Frankly, will you? Dad needs them."

"Coming," said Ott, and she began climbing down.

Pinchton sighed. Was he never to learn the mystery of the Thudding Thing That Snarls? He swallowed the last chip and swung down after her.

In the garden, Mr Primm was talking to Mrs Weird about bikes. He had had a Harley-Davidson himself as a lad, so he said. How totally amazing. As Pinchton passed, he heard Mrs Weird offering to let him have a go. His father looked quite excited.

Mrs Primm was telling Mr Weird how clever he was to have a son so keen to do his homework. Mr Weird gave a polite bow and offered her another stuffed tomato.

Things were going really well. How strange.

In fact, thought Pinchton, it didn't matter that he hadn't found out all the secrets yet. There was plenty of time. He knew that, from now on, he was going to be seeing a *lot* of the Weirds.

In the middle of the night, he sat bolt upright in bed and clapped a hand to his head. An awful thought had struck him.

He knew where the tomatoes had come from!

Barrington Stoke would like to thank all its readers for commenting on the manuscript before publication and in particular:

Thomas Barclay
Jenny Bristow
Sarah Brown
Angela Campbell
Ailie Crerar
Nicole Ferguson
Andrew Fulton
Michael A. Galloway
Jenny Gooch
Stewart Kennedy
Hannah Le Masurier
Amil Mair
Johnathon McCreadie
James Alexander McKenzie
Amy Lauren Middlemiss
Lyn Middlemiss
Jennifer Murray
Conor Nicolson
Mary Nicolson
Vicky Norris
Jack Pryor
Hamish Patrick Rowe
Lyn Sellward
Freddie Slessor
Margaret Smith
Lisa Tenzin-Dolma
Amber Tenzin-Dolma
Emily Thomson
Jourdan Whitefoot
Andrew Wight
Ana-Maria Wilson
Angela Wilson
Ciara Wilson
Martin Wright

Become a Consultant!

Would you like to give us feedback on our titles before they are published? Contact us at the email address below – we'd love to hear from you!

info@barringtonstoke.co.uk
www.barringtonstoke.co.uk